Frogness

Written by
Sarah Nelson

Illustrated by
Eugenie Fernandes

Owlkids Books

Just before dusk,
rain clouds bloom
way out over the sea.

We wait.

Behind the house,
in the muddy marsh,

it starts.

Yeep,
   yeep,
      yeep!

Chocolate yips.
He nips at my shirt.

"Wanna try again?" I ask.

So sweatshirt on
and out we go—
out under the moon
and the first winking stars—

tiptoeing,
barefoot,
as the chorus grows.

Tonight, we're sure to catch one.

I can hear them everywhere—
millions, probably—

croaking and chirping
and clucking and burping.

It is SO loud!

I can't hear the sea
or the wind in the leaves
or if my mother is calling me.

My head is full of frogs.

We wriggle under bushes
and sneak through reeds
and rushes.

No frogs.

We crawl across a fallen tree,
hang over the sides
and try to see.

No frogs.

We creep, creep along the creek,
mucking through the mush—

***squish, squoosh*—**

poking between cattails,
peeking under stones
and leaves
and logs . . .

Still,
no frogs.

**Where are
they hiding?!**

Chocolate and I
flop down in the grass
and give up searching.

No thinking.
Just being.
We fade off into frogness …

RUUUuuUup, RUUUuuUup,
RUUUuuUup, RUUUuuUup!

Brrrrraaap, brrrrraaap,
brrrrraaap, brrrrraaap!

Yeep-yeep-yeep-yeep-
yeep-yeep-yeep-yeep!

We melt into that song—

and float like frogs
on lily pads
over the pond
in pieces of the setting sun.

Ahhhh . . .

But then—

PLINK!

I hold my breath
and slowly …
slowly …

WRROOOFFF!

The frog
leaps—

long-legged,
into the pond.

Plop!

All at once,
from everywhere—
frogs come flying!

Big ones,
small ones,
fat ones,
long ones—

Plop!

Plop! Plop!

Plop! Plop!

Plop!

Plop!

Chocolate smacks the water,
belly first.

Frogs scatter.
We splash and splatter.

Chocolate almost gets
a taste of frog legs!

I think I have one,
but **zzlip**—
it's through my fingers.

Gone.

They're just too fast!

At last, we sit,
toes dipped in—
grinning.

All around us,
the frog marsh
sings.

We're hunt happy
and bone
weary.

But from somewhere at the
edge of frogness,

I can hear my mother calling.

"Saaammmy!"

And so …

we leapfrog home—
hip-hop over stumps
and over stones.

At the door, Mom calls us frogcakes.
She points to the garden hose.

"Leave the swamp outside, please."

Then she wraps us up
in warm towels
and rubs our wet hair dry.

Deep in the night,
while we sleep,
it rains.

I must still hear
the frog marsh singing,
because I dream I'm swimming
through a blue-black sky
of lily pads.

And in my head,
and in my heart,
everywhere, everywhere …
are frogs
and stars
and pieces of moon.

A CHORUS OF FROGS

There are almost 7,000 species—or different kinds—of frogs living all around the world. Most frogs live in watery places like streams and marshes. But others live in trees, meadows, and even deserts. Frogs come in many colors and sizes. Some tropical frogs are flashy red or electric blue. The tiniest frogs are pea-sized. The biggest, the goliath frog of West Africa, can grow more than a foot (30 cm) long and weigh as much as a small dog. However, most frogs are brown or green and rather small. They often look remarkably like the mud, rocks, or leaves of the places where they live.

Though it can be difficult to see frogs—and even more difficult to *catch* one—we can't help but hear their wonderful and strange calls. Some frog calls sound like croaking, belching, or even snoring. Other frogs sound like ducks quacking, pigs snorting, crickets chirping, or woodpeckers tapping on a tree trunk. Every species of frog has its own unique call. And many species have a somewhat different call depending on where they live. Like people, frogs have accents!

A frog calls with its mouth closed, pushing air back and forth between its lungs and mouth. Stretchy skin, called a vocal sac, puffs up like a balloon beneath its mouth. Even a very small frog can make a giant sound. Some frog calls can be heard a *mile* (1.6 km) away.

Like you, frogs make noise for all kinds of reasons. They call to protect their space, to warn one another of danger, to attract a mate, and often before a rainstorm. Many frogs are nocturnal, and so we especially hear them calling at night. When frogs sing together . . . it's a frog chorus.

*For Sylvia, Val, and Thea,
whose littler selves helped
inspire this story —S.N.*

For Janice and Jane —E.F.

———————————

A special thanks to my Minnesota
writing friends who helped me find the
heart and soul of *Frogness* and to
Dr. Mike Benard for his insights
regarding frog calls —*S.N.*

Owlkids Books acknowledges the financial support of the Canada Council for the Arts,
the Ontario Arts Council, the Government of Canada through the Canada Book Fund
(CBF), and the Government of Ontario through the Ontario Creates Book Initiative
for our publishing activities.

Published in Canada by Owlkids Books Inc., 1 Eglinton Avenue East, Toronto, ON, M4P 3A1

Published in the US by Owlkids Books Inc., 1700 Fourth Street, Berkeley, CA, 94710

Library of Congress Control Number: 2020940654

Library and Archives Canada Cataloguing in Publication

Title: Frogness / written by Sarah Nelson ; illustrated by Eugenie Fernandes.
Names: Nelson, Sarah, 1973- author. | Fernandes, Eugenie, 1943- illustrator.
Identifiers: Canadiana 20200275038 | ISBN 9781771473750 (hardcover)
Classification: LCC PZ7.1.N45 Fro 2021 | DDC j813/.6—dc23

Edited by Karen Li & Karen Boersma | Designed by Alisa Baldwin

Manufactured in Guangdong Province, Dongguan City, China, in November 2020,
by Toppan Leefung Packaging & Printing (Dongguan) Co., Ltd.
Job #BAYDC87

A   B   C   D   E   F

Publisher of Chirp, Chickadee and OWL
www.owlkidsbooks.com

Owlkids Books is a division of bayard canada